I0747454

"Don't try to resist her, take the ride or better yet, let Garcia's poems ride and take you over. A.L. Garcia is the Powerful Erotic Poetess that we have been waiting. Erica Jong once wrote: 'The corruption begins with the mouth, the tongue, the wanting.' The first poem in the world is I want to eat. Don't just nibble or take bites, let Garcia's poems swallow you whole. I urge you to savor the tasty sensual feast of *My Split Tongue//Mi Lengua Dividida*, again and again."

— ADRIAN ERNESTO CEPEDA,
AUTHOR OF LA LENGUA INSIDE ME
AND WE ARE THE ONES POSSESSED

"A haunting collection that reads like bloody fingerprints left on the skin. *Una perspectiva hechizante, ricamente imaginativa y hermosa.*"

— JESSIKA GREWE GLOVER, AUTHOR
OF BLOODLILY AND THE ANOTHER
BEAST'S SKIN SERIES

"Alma Garcia is a true poet, an elegant linguist to take note of. *My Split Tongue // Mi Lengua Dividida* is an incantation, forcing out an inner goddess to the surface. It's a love letter to everything you've ever loved and lost. A breathtaking account of brutal vulnerability that will penetrate the soul. The most beautiful collection you'll read this year."

— ALYSSA ALESSI, AUTHOR OF IZZY
HOFFMAN IS NOT A WITCH

"Garcia's riveting words gather you into a poetic unearthly trance, taking you on a flight through visceral emotion. A sensual storytelling intertwined with verses that beautifully haunt the reader. A must read that will keep you captivated and riveted to the pages within."

— ANN MARIE ELEAZER, AUTHOR OF
SHE'S MAGIC AND MIDNIGHT LACE

my split tongue // mi lengua
dividida

my split tongue // mi lengua dividida

A BILINGUAL COLLECTION

A.L. GARCIA

My Split Tongue // Mi Lengua Dividida:
a bilingual collection
written by A.L. Garcia
published by Quill & Crow Publishing House

Cover Design by Fay Lane

Interior by Cassandra L. Thompson

Printed in the United States of America

ISBN (ebook) 978-1-958228-93-7

ISBN (print) 978-1-958228-94-4

Publisher's Website: quillandcrowpublishinghouse.com

for the butchered tongues that live within our spirits yet
...and the will to keep them
a las lenguas masacradas que viven en nuestras
almas aún
...y la voluntad de conservarlas

introduction

Spanish is my first language, my mother tongue, *una matriz.* Portuguese is my second. English is my third, born of migration, of things both lost and won. Italian is the fourth language I learned, thanks to a Catholic Saturday school and the promise of cannoli at the end of the week. Latin comes from searching for the root. French, I'm just dipping my feet in. Quechua is a tongue owned of an ancestry I did not get to see grow old. This collection hails from those many butchered tongues, those many experiences, voices I have sometimes quieted but never forgotten. They have come to me with unbridled passion in this collection, like arrows through my breast, and I only hope I have done them justice.

- A.L. Garcia, Puerto Rico, 2025

my split tongue

MI LENGUA DIVIDIDA

prose

PROSA

give me back my tongue

(MARIANGULA)

The girls sit cuddled on the loveseat, whispering in one another's ears and giggling to themselves as the skin on their thighs alternates between clinging to and slipping over the plastic-covered florals beneath their grandmother Emiliana's gaze. Her rocking chair groans as she sways back and forth, cupping a mugful of lemongrass tea in her small, papery hands. Emiliana takes a sip and leans forward, scanning their mischievous eyes, their innocent smiles...sips...grins...

"A story before supper,
ven (come)
I'm going to tell you the story of Mariangula."

The girls scurry to the floor near the rocking chair, huddling together once again.
Emiliana leans in further, whispering ominously,

Once upon a time, a great misfortune fell over the land, a wasting disease, a terrible plague that would destroy you from the inside out, **eat you alive!** No one knew exactly how or why the plague came, but they had stories, rumors. And rumors spread, are always spreading, especially during times of misfortune. How many of them are true, no one knows, but that never stops them from spreading. My mother—your great grandmother—would say rumors are like snakes. They crawl in through cracks, hide in crevices, and shed their skin as they grow and shift until they get big enough to suffocate you, consuming you whole.

Some said that the wasting was a curse that came to punish the greed of men, their consumption, their gluttony. Others claimed it was the work of the devil himself, that demons would possess the spirit of those who tempted them, would sit on their bellies when they slept, and suck their spirits right out along with their flesh. Some said it just came from eating too much pan dulce, *like you two do!*

The girls shriek playfully as Emiliana chuckles in satisfaction and goes on.

The more people were infected, the more the rumors grew. The people were full of fear, the rumors like snakes in their bellies. One day, a young woman named Mariangula came from a neighboring land with new stories, ideas, tinctures, and herbal remedies to stop the spread of the disease. But she was not often met kindly. Some even called her an omen of the plague. Some called her a witch, *una bruja.*

The girls blurt out in unison,

"Why did they call her those things?"

Emiliana shushes them.

There has never been a shortage of reasons to call a woman a witch. But, in Mariangula's case, it was simply her tongue, her ideas. Mariangula claimed the plague could be traced back to the farms, to the animals, how they were kept, and how they were prepared for consumption. She had made it her mission in life to spread the word, to warn others of what she had seen, had learned through experience, to prevent spread of the plague that had left her without a family, without a home. As the sole survivor of her family, of her land, she believed she had been spared for this purpose, for truth, for change.

The first to receive her were those who were suffering from the wasting themselves, desperate for solutions, or those who, like her, had survived but lost their loved ones, their livelihood. She made tinctures and stews to ease their suffering, recipes passed down to her from her mother and her mother's mother before her. Some said that she was a healer. Others condemned her, but she stayed true to her mission, to the hope that the truth would prevail.

Then, one evening, Mariangula was called on by a wealthy widower, a cattle farmer named Don Miguel. Don Miguel had already lost his wife to the wasting disease, and now his young daughter had fallen ill. She was all he had left for family, and he would spare no expense in her treatment. But it was to no avail. Mariangula, with her so-called brujeria (magic), was his last resort. She went to him willingly. She almost expected his call. She willed it so. After examining his daughter, Mariangula spoke to Don Miguel privately.

"I do not know what you have heard of me, Don Miguel, but I will warn you, I am no magician. I have lost my own family to the wasting, but my mother worked with herbs and taught me their uses before she passed. I have noticed some may be effective against the progression of the plague. I will try my best to ease your daughter's suffering, but I can make no promises. All I ask in return is for temporary quarters and the chance to examine the cattle as well."

Don Miguel agreed. "You have my word."

Mariangula tended to the daughter as if she were her own child, and the girl soon began showing signs of improvement, growth. Don Miguel's interest in Mariangula grew too, right alongside his daughter's health. For months, he watched the enchantress work, reveling in her discoveries, her experiments, her lines of questioning, her manner, her stews, her knowledge. He made it a habit of accompanying when she toiled over her cauldrons, and they had long conversations he grew quite fond of, missed when she was gone. For months, he gave in to her demands and implemented her changes around the farm in spite of the rumors brought about by her presence. But he had a plan.

The girls stare wide-eyed, like deer caught in headlights. Emiliana leans in again.

"So what do you think he will do? Hmm...?"

The girls are enraptured. They howl in protest as Emiliana pauses, stands, and walks to the kitchen to prepare herself another cup of tea.

"Hey! What happens next? Please! We want to know!"

Their grandmother chortles as she responds,

"I'll be right back."

The living room is pitch black. The light filtering in from the kitchen doorway makes strange shadows on the walls. The girls huddle closer to one another, interlace their fingers.

"What do you think will happen next?"

"...I don't know..."

Emiliana returns from the kitchen with her mug in one hand and two pan dulces in the other. She settles back in her rocking chair and hands the treats to the girls.

"Eat."

She continues.

> He would marry her! He was certain a holy union would shift rumors in his favor. She was bound to find the cause of the wasting...it was only a matter of time. The popularity of her stews was not lost on him. Together, they would rid the land of the wasting and build an empire! That night, he called for her and waited for her at the garden entrance beneath the full moon with a bouquet of wildflowers. He had caught her admiring them one day. She was startled when she first saw him on account of his unusual behavior but brushed it off and greeted him as usual. "Good evening, Miguel."
> He stuttered, unsure of himself, but found his confidence, "Mariangula, mmm...I know this may come as a surprise, but I think it would benefit us both greatly if you would agree to...to marry me. My daughter loves you. You saved her when no one else could. You will save us all.

You. You were my...my last hope. Now, I can't stop thinking of you and what we could do together. Stay with us. Marry me. You will want of nothing. I promise you."

A tear streams from Emiliana's left eye, a remnant of something lost, a memory...

The girls gasp in anticipation.

Mariangula was frozen where she stood. Her tongue weighed in tons. She wanted to say, "I do not want of anything. I must continue my mission when I am done here. I cannot stay here." But she couldn't bring herself to move, to speak.

He took her silence as permission, as acceptance. He took her hand in his, pressed his body close to hers, crushing the wildflowers under his arm, and repeated, "Tell me you have felt it, too...this desire." He craned his neck down to kiss her. Her body awakened. She recoiled from his alien touch and shoved him away, her voice simultaneously breaking free from its prison of flesh and rolling violently off her tongue,

"No! I...I don't...I...I want nothing from you. I am sorry. Please...Please forgive me. I...I don't need anything from you."

The rejection crashed over Miguel like a tidal wave. He couldn't believe his ears. No one said no to him. His knees buckled, and she reached out to steady him, extending her hand, her sympathy betraying her. He took the opportunity to seize her in his arms. He squeezed her by the shoulders. "No. I CHOOSE YOU! Don't you understand? I have done everything you have asked of me! I have tolerated rumors! I've done everything right, everything you could ask of a man! I deserve you! I deserve this!"

Mariangula could feel her rage bubbling within, but still, she pleaded with him, "Please, stop, let me go; think of your daughter," but Don Miguel showed no restraint, no mercy. She tried to speak again, but he wrapped his hands around her throat, silencing her.

His fingers dug into her supple skin, satisfying his ego, his wound. He squeezed harder, suffocating her. "I did everything right! How dare you do this to me! How dare you deny me! Witch! I will never let you go! Never!"

The girls cry out horrified, flashing her glimpses of the chewed-up pan dulce on their tongues. She shushes them gently while tapping a finger on their chin to remind them of their manners.

Mariangula's body thrashed against his grip. He was a possessed man—proud, invincible, omnipotent, a god of skin and bone and ire. And yet, he remained no match for her. She was a woman, a will, a wilderness, an incarnation. Her tongue sprang forth, a Leviathan in her defense. It wrapped around his throat, constricting on contact, crushing his esophagus in seconds. He choked, his eyes bulging from his skull, his regret in tears of blood trickling onto her tongue. He didn't get to see his daughter as she entered the garden, didn't get to hear her screams of terror at the sight of him and Mariangula wrapped in their gruesome embrace.

All across the land, the winds carried the horror, the tragedy of her tongue, of Mariangula, his greed releasing the gluttony of the wasting...a knock at their doors...

...an echo in the wind...

...Mariangula.

"*Devuelveme mi lengua,* give me back my tongue," it said.

All across the night, the people stood paralyzed, unable to speak, to scream, to move, anchored in place at their bedsides. Their mouths hung open, stretching wider and wider, wider than ever. Blood stained their cheeks as their tongues grew a life of their own. The tongues slipped past their lips, further and further out, split as they descended, the bifurcated factions slithering like snakes down their sides. The wind whispered again, in her voice...

...the voice of her tragedy...

"*Devuelveme mi lengua*...give me back my tongue," it said.

The tongue-snakes flooded the streets, carrying the entrails of their owners along with them, leaving behind nothing but husks of who they once were, who they once aimed to be.

The doorbell rings. It's followed by knocking.

...a whisper in the wind...

The girls shriek again. Their grandmother cackles.

"Oh hush, it's just your mother...

...go get the door."

————*END*

lula and the girl with

no name

(ALMA)

They were of the wind and the wild...
She was of the moon

We sit in a circle around the embers of a dying fire, my gaze darting from one pair of eyes to the next, scanning the gaunt, grimy faces for any sign of impending deception. *The wilderness is not made for the unsuspicious.* I furrow my brow as I reach the strays, a pair of emaciated blondes found earlier about two thousand paces due south of the ruins.

Their big, pea-green eyes remind me of the dried sphagnum moss bunched up in my pocket. My stomach growls. I reach for the moss, rip a piece off, and tuck it into the corner of my mouth. It will ward off the hunger—the beast—for a while. I start toward them, my resolve renewed.

The blondes shift nervously under my glare as I make my way over to them and gesture for them to follow me. I lead them to a small shelter camouflaged by layers of pine branches in between two large oaks. The oak twins, I call them, for the way their roots grow into each other. I hand one the remaining moss. They do not speak our language, but I speak nonetheless.

"Hoc tene."
(hold this)

Keeping my gaze on them, I reach inside my shelter. I notice their breathing slow down as they see my heavy water-skin, their hammering heartbeats betraying the cold, dead look in their olive eyes. In one seamless move, I drop the water-skin, grab my hunting dagger, and hurry into a fighting stance. I growl under my breath.

...aut necare."
(or be killed)

The taller one falls to his knees with his hands up, then tugs at the tattered shirt of the shorter one. The youngling stands defiant, the scant moonlight filtering through the canopies gleaming in his verdant eyes.

He is like most strays we encounter these days, concerned with what they need, what they can take. Nothing more.

My stomach growls again, the beast within hot in my breast now. The small one lunges, the taller one on his heels.

I react as I always do, my whole miserable existence flashing before my eyes as every movement blends instinctually into the next. I lean forward into the shorter one's attack, plunging the dagger into the soft meat of his underbelly. His body folds over me as I tighten my grip and twist the knife before dragging it across his hips, disemboweling the unfortunate. I push him off me in the direction of the other boy and grimace as his blood and viscera spill over my arm, torso, and face. What remains of him falls into the hands of the older one as I stand to face him. He gathers them to his chest and shrieks,

"NO! Kaleb! NO!"

I pause, raptured in a sudden memory.

A name.

A blur of voices and faces race through my mind, obscuring my senses. Tears streaming, his face in a distortion, he charges at me. I'm tackled to the ground in my stupor and feel his cold, bony hands wrap around my throat.

"I'M GOING TO KILL YOU, BITCH!"

I catch glimpses of the world around me as my eyes roll back into my skull. The whole pack is surrounding us now, silently waiting for a victor or for no victor or simply for more death. I close my eyes, wrap my fingers around his wrists, my legs around his waist. I squeeze, channeling all my energy into my thighs and my grip until I hear his bones give way to the pressure. I squeeze harder, waiting for the familiar *crunch* of victory.

He wails in agony as his grip on my throat loosens. I stand and shake myself free as he falls to the ground in a heap. My jaws unhinge instinctually, stretching and contorting my lips, the skin at the corners of my mouth, my cheeks, as the moss inside trickles out pathetically...

...I cry out,

"Aut neca aut necare!"
(kill or be killed)

The pack howls in unison as we continue to shift, our soft faces stretching thin over the large maws growing beneath. The broken boy at our feet stares wide-eyed, paralyzed by his fear, his mouth agape. I can see he is trying to scream again, *not that it would do any good out here.* We loom over him now, our short limbs having nearly doubled in size as we transform.

They grow more beast with every shift.

The boy shivers uncontrollably, clinging desperately to the spilled guts of his twin, and soils himself. I can smell his terror in it. I almost feel bad for him. I lean down to face him as the others lick their teeth in anticipation, their claws still pushing through their fingertips, their horns still ripping through their hair. I lift his head up with one razor-sharp talon beneath his chin as his survival instincts kick in. He mutters through his tears.

"Please...stop..."

I cut his mumbling off in one swift movement, my claw nearly decapitating him as it impales his jugular. I pull up, completing the motion, and the only sound left in him is the blood spewing from the wound.

It's for the better, I tell myself.

At least his suffering is over.

I tangle my talons into his straw hair and raise the head high for all to see. The tongue of the beast spills from between my fangs, lapping at the blood dripping from the dead boy's chin. It splits in two, and the bifurcated sections travel up his face, forcing themselves through his eye sockets.

The beast wanted those wildgrass eyes from the moment it met them. The beast always takes what it wants.

Once its grotesque ritual is over, I drop the skull to the ground, take a deep breath, and speak to the group again.

"Memento Doloris."
(Remember the Pain)

They howl in agreement as they lunge at the corpses. I howl back at them, then stagger away, slipping into the safety of my shelter and leaving them to their morbid devices.

I am tired. I am so, so tired.

I curl up at the base of the oak twins again and shut my eyes, recalling what little memories remain of my child-self back to me. The beast protests against me. The strange, cruel body convulses in reaction, and burns hot with its rage. It is getting harder and harder to come back from these shifts. I manage it once again.

But I am tired. I am so tired.

I drag my hands across my restored face and sigh. It is thinner than it was before. It sags more. I am weak, but I can't let anyone see that.

The pack.

They grow stronger by the day. They are bolder than me. Faster. More welcoming of their...gift...curse...whatever it is. All the remnants of the children they once were are gone. I am lost. I do not know what I have become. What they have become.

What are we? What am I?

I have heard some who are brave enough, quick enough to speak intelligibly call us beasts. I don't remember what that actually means. I know we are not exactly human anymore. But we are also not just beast. We are something in between. Something worse than them, perhaps.

We are children of inhumanity,
our own human inhumanity.
We are their monsters now.
As they were ours.
Are ours.

The thoughts tormenting me are not exactly a lullaby. But still, I sleep.

I wake at the witching hour like I always do, surrounded by complete darkness. I know it will dawn in a few hours. I still follow the moon when I remember to. She helps me keep track of time and direction. She is to the far east of us now. Her light is a welcome comfort in the almost permanent gloom of the dense canopies.

I look around again. The pack cleaned up the mess well. Their bellies are full, and they are fast asleep. I can hear their breathing, slow and steady. And their stomachs digesting, gurgling. They look like my friends when they are sleeping, like my pack, like family. My eyes well up with tears. I paw at them. I remember a feeling used to follow. Before. But not anymore.

Now, I am hollow.
A crow caws in the distance.

I look up, squinting my eyes to catch a glimpse of it, but see instead a large sylphlike figure soaring high above the edge of the trees. Another beast, perhaps, I think to myself. But a beautiful one, at least. I rub my eyes, look up again, and see her still.

It is as if she were flying towards the moon. She reaches the crescent and descends, her shadowy figure almost evanescing beneath the silver sickle. My eyes remain fixated on the spot until I hear a twig snap behind me. I turn, but there is nothing.

The wind whistling through the trees is my only companion. It is time to go.

I leave my shelter in place between the twin oaks, taking nothing with me. In spite of the beasts within, I remember having loved and known most of the pack since they were babes. I don't remember exactly how or when we came into the forest, but I remember being chased. I remember my mother. I remember her running deeper and deeper into the wild with me in her arms. I remember her persisting until her toes bled and her legs failed her. I remember her curling up with me at the base of the twin oaks...

...dying there.
I remember her warm body turning cold around me, rigid...
...and then limp again
...and then putrid.
I remember...
...the flies
...the maggots
...and the children
scattered like dandelion seeds across the vast, wet, green, and black abyss.
lost
crying out for their mothers
for anyone
for...
...me

I remember my own tears, my own grief...but I can't feel them anymore, not since I grew my teeth.

I don't feel anything now.
I remember the feelings, but I don't feel them.
I remember losing them, losing myself,
in little pieces, some days carved from my side, others filleted
from my thighs.
Sometimes chewed off like the memory of biting into an apple,
or picking a cherry from a tree.

Remembering was equal parts gift and curse. And everyone seemed free of it now, but me.

Memento Doloris
(Remember the Pain)

I don't remember my name. No one remembers their name, but even if we did, it wouldn't matter.

Nothing matters now.
We are children of our human inhumanity.
We are their monsters.
As they were ours.
Are ours.

I look around at our home, knowing exactly where each shelter is camouflaged. I pause, then turn away. I turn my hand up toward the moon at an angle, making an L with it. I line my index finger up with the horns of the crescent moon and find the path I will take. The salty wetness streams down my face again as I slip away from the camp toward the moonlight.

I move more swiftly than I have in a long time, unencumbered by responsibility, by guilt. I cover my tracks, knowing I have taught them too well for my own good, knowing they will come for me, too, once they realize I'm gone.

My stomach growls. My lips ache with thirst. The beast demands to be heard. The persistent child silences it.

Aut inveniam viam aut faciam.
(I shall find a way or make one)

I keep going until exhaustion sets in. Then crawl into a hollow at the base of a giant sequoia, just as dark clouds begin to consume the evening sky, curling myself into a fetal position to sleep. I remember my mother's arms around me.

In the morning, I wake to the sound of voices in the distance. I messed up. I got too comfortable. I slept in.

I have to move.

I look around, catching a glimpse of a black willow to the east and take off sprinting.

The ground is moist and slippery from the storm. I stumble as I reach a muddy ravine, unable to stop myself from rolling down towards the stream. I end up on my hands and knees at the base of the ravine covered in sludge. I crawl over to the water's edge, looking down to see a haunted, grim reflection staring back at me.

Is that me?

I strike at the water to make it go away, then cup some in

my hands and splash it onto my face, attempting to collect myself, my thoughts. The unexpected sound of hissing startles me. I stand and start backing away from the water.

Snakes.

Hundreds of them, thousands maybe, emerge from the stream, slithering towards me as I turn and run.

Memories flood my skull, blinding me. The feelings come back like waves of a tumultuous sea, overpowering all my senses. I stumble again, landing hard on my knees and forearms. I lay there, ready to give up.

What am I surviving for?

A crow circles the sky above me, cawing vociferously.

I lift my head up, noticing we are in a clearing. I must be dreaming. There are no clearings in these woods. I look back at the trees, then forward. There is a small cottage in the distance, standing alone in the middle of the clearing. I watch as the crow flies over to it, perches on the roof, then flies away. I pick myself up and walk over to the cottage. I feel like I am floating. I wonder if I'm dead.

I knock at the door, remembering the courtesy.

"Hello."

A short, round-faced, old woman with silver hair opens the door. She greets me.

"Welcome, my child, we have been expecting you."

I cock my head in confusion.

"Expecting me?
Who are you?
Am I alive?"

The old woman smiles.

"I am Lula.
Yes, you are alive.
Come inside."

I follow her into the cottage, where a wooden table is adorned with a feast of freshly fried fish, assorted fruits, nuts, and chocolates. I close my eyes and breathe in the scent of the household.

This can't be real, but I don't care.

I hear a door creak and glare in the direction of the sound. An old man walks in from a garden. He smiles and gestures to the table.

"You are hungry. You will need strength.
Please.
Eat."

I eat. I think I have died. Perhaps I am dreaming. I look over to the kind strangers when I finish. They are sitting at the table watching me. I wipe my mouth, clear my throat, and question them again:

"Who are you?
What are you?"

Lula turns her gaze to mine and replies solemnly,

"We are you.

"We have been lost in the wild for longer than you know,
longer than you accept. Time stands still in these woods, see.
And the beasts keep us here. They lie. They lie because they
need us, our bodies. They make us think we can't leave, that we
are weak, that we can't survive without them. But that is not
true."

I furrow my brow at her, my beast biting back.

"And you, where is your beast?
If you are me..."

Lula chuckles at its snark and snaps back.

"Quiet..."

She starts toward me. My body tenses with foresight and
duality. The child and the beast. They fight for me, my body,
my mind, my soul. The beast thrashes. The persistent child
holds still. She places the palm of her hand over my forehead
and begins a prayer, an incantation.

"Vos a luna es, semper
of the moon you are, of the moon, you will always be

semper liber
free, you shall always be
you will sleep and rise
cum libertate, liber
with freedom, free
and your name will be
Alma.
"Now it is time for you to rest. You will need your strength.
Somnium.
Dream."

She waves her hand over me, and my eyelids grow heavy as lead. I feel myself drifting off into a peaceful slumber as Lula cradles me in her arms. I let myself collapse into her bosom and dream of places I have never known, never seen, of the sea, just beyond the horizon.

I know where I have to go, what I have to do.

When she wakes, the cottage is gone. She is alone, face down in the middle of the clearing. She stands, looks back at the wilderness, and makes out two small figures through the trees, looming over another. As she rubs her eyes and waits for them to focus, a voice within whispers.

The pack.

She starts toward them. They look up at her, startle, then turn and run into the trees. She picks up the scent of death and turns away...

*breathes in the wind that blows in from the horizon, tastes it
on her tongue...
...salt.
And runs.*

———— End

fly me to the moon

(AMBER)

He is an insect who dreamt he was a man.
The dream is over now.

Summer in the tropics comes with rainstorms and a humidity that makes the air impossibly dense. The ceiling fan whirs begrudgingly through the warmth of an environment Amber is still unaccustomed to. It isn't just the climate either. August tends to turn her thoughts into molasses regardless of the weather. Tonight renders her particularly useless, her eyes glued to the hypnotizing twirling of the blades as she lies there naked, motionless, a corpse spread over the damp white sheets. She can't sleep. There is nothing behind her eyelids but the sorrow of everything left behind, of loss, of him.

This won't last forever. Nothing lasts forever. Nothing.

She closes her eyes, and lets her mind drift.

Thinking of him, of them, of life, of death
Adán

She doesn't even need her hands to roam, her fingers to explore. Her imagination, her reflexes are enough, more than enough. Her thoughts twitch with memories of his eyes on her, conjuring his touch, his need, makes fantasies that throb beneath her skin, swell in her veins, fill her from the inside out, make her whole. Her desire is a spell of longing, a manifestation of his flesh, his ghost. She whispers or thinks of whispering.

ven
(come)
ven aqui
(come here)
ven a mi
(come to me)

There is a fly on the wall, and all he can do is spy on her, watch her like she watches that damned ceiling fan, watch her fucking herself in her bed, in her head, over and over again, watch her writhing there, calling for someone he doesn't know, doesn't remember. A multitude of powerful compound eyes take in every angle, every curve of her anatomy, every detail of her skin, every twitch of the muscles beneath. He can almost taste her sweat, her blood, her wetness, her need, just by the scent of it, sweet, so sweet, like honey. He longs for it like he's never longed for anything before, to be trapped in her, to be an insect in Amber.

He would die for a taste of it, of life, of her. Oh, how he

wants her, how he longs to be a corpse over that bare landscape, that blank page of possibility, over her. Death or whatever it is that lies ahead would be a small price to pay, and damn whatever it affects.

*He is reckless, fearless, apolitical,
a fly on the fucking wall.*

She is nearly a puddle now, her lips parting in anticipation of another climax, her throat releasing its pleasure in desperate, breathy moans, gasping for the syrupy air of the night as she grips the bed sheets. He calculates the distance, the risk, the absurdity of it all, if only for a moment before the fall. He swoops down, careful not to startle her, and lands gently on her mound just as she coats throbbing flesh in her cream once more. He salivates, his own ecstasy dripping out of him along with hers, making her his, blending her with his world, his spit. He sucks it all up for her as her mind stills, her ragged breaths turn back to quiet ones, as her heartbeat normalizes until it's as normal as it can get.

Until he is just a fly on the fucking wall again.

Morning comes with a pounding to the skull—it sounds like someone's taking a battering ram to the door. The Catholic in her reprimands her for being so fruitless throughout the night, for spending it in her head again, in her indecency. It speaks in the voice of her aunt, a Carmelite nun in Barcelona. She runs her hands through coarse, dark hair, tugging at it gently and forcing a deep, cleansing breath.

Confession: Silence is a terrible thing to get accustomed to.

"Amber! Damn it! Open up!"

Zoe.

The pounding wasn't only in her head after all. She lazily slips on a pair of white panties and a tank top as she tumbles towards the front door.

"I'm coming! I'm coming!—I'm sorry!"

Zoe bounces into the warehouse-turned-lab full speed ahead. The minute she unlocks the door, carrying on about a fundraiser she will surely end up dragging them to, Amber recoils at the sunlight trailing her. She closes the door behind her and locks it.

"Hold on, please. Coffee. I need coffee."

Zoe pauses like a train stopped in her tracks, looking over at her.

"How are you?"

Amber looks back at her. Her eyes were moss-covered marbles, full of worry, the color of forests at midday and river water in the sunlight. She stares at them, her own dark orbs muddling in rapture with the kind of attention one can only give to things unknown or lost, and forces a smile.

"I'm good. I promise."

Zoe squints.

"I'll make coffee. And put some music on, ok?"

Amber grins genuinely.

"Thank you."

Zoe beams and bounces away towards the kitchen as Amber trudges over to her disaster of a research desk, anxiety on her heels, and begins rummaging through a pile for the notes on her latest experiment. She finds it, scans it, crumples it, closes her eyes, sighs, mutters under her breath,

"A bigger storm, more lightning, more power..."

Zoe's playlist and the scent of freshly brewed caffeine fills the studio.

"Fly me to the moon..."
Sinatra

She closes her eyes, breathes in, breathes out...
Zoe clears a spot on the desk, replacing chaos with a steaming mugful of the miracle bean water.
Zoe reaches out to her.

"Want to dance?"

She takes her hand, rising from the chair into a twirl, into her arms. Zoe grabs her by the waist with the grace of a stream, the same placid rivers in her eyes as she completes the turn, her free hand tucking Amber's dark hair behind her ear.

"Everything will be alright. The storm nears. *Ven.* Come here."

Amber smirks, pulling Zoe into a slow waltz as the rhythm of the song replaces the anxiety in her feet, her hips, the voices in her head.

He is a fly on the fucking wall.

All he can do is spy on her, watch her, drive himself mad with envy, dream himself a man, a corpse, anything but a fly on the wall, anything but what he is. The insect in him doesn't understand what happened, why he feels the way he does, why he feels at all.

Something is wrong.
Something is terribly wrong.

Consciousness, manhood, knowledge, lust, fear, want, need—all of it. They flood the cells of the inadequate insect shell, threatening apotheosis, not so spontaneous combustion, aching to rip him apart, to send him flying through the air in chunks. He can almost taste it on his tongue— humanity—the blood, so much blood, puddles, plasma, pools, and pools of it. They course through him like an ocean, like rain, like thunderstorms, like silent lightning, whispering things through the static—collect calls from a designer telephone booth...

"an insect that dreamt he was a man"

...ringing

...running out of time.

What is the lifespan of a fly?

The doorbell chimes. A voice from the other side rings out,

"I've got an urgent delivery here for Eden Laboratories from the Hospital Metropolitano."

Amber's face lights up. She rushes to the closet for her lab coat and slips it on over the tank top like an alternate skin, a face in which she can face the world. She greets the delivery man at the door with a customary, brief smile.

"Buenos días, Antonio!"

The young man smiles back generously,

"Doctora, buenos días! How has the weather been treating you?"

She wrinkles her nose at his routine small talk,

"Hmm. It's been a little hot, but I'm holding up."

He chuckles, handing her a tablet with digital release forms,

"Ah sí, el calor ha sido infernal...es verdad
(oh yes, the heat has been infernal, it's true)...but we are
expecting storms that should cool things down a bit.
You should come to the Hacienda this weekend after the
fundraiser. It'll be fun."

She takes the familiar device, quickly scans the inventory page, and returns her gaze to him.

"Oh, the storm sounds divine and thank you for the invite. I'll think about it. I'll meet you around the back, ok?"

He nods in confirmation and turns from her towards a white van parked a couple of feet away. She turns back inside, her face in the tablet, and asks Zoe to open the back gate. Zoe skips over to the back entrance of the facility and down a hallway that leads to their "cold rooms," two heavily insulated container bays Amber had shipped in from their original lab. She shivers with nostalgia as she passes the insulated doors, running her hands up and down her arms in a poor attempt to shield herself from the memories stealthily filtering through them.

She reaches the loading dock at the end of the hall and enters her security code into the gate operator, grateful for the sunlight and wave of heat that comes pouring in as the heavy steel rises. Antonio comes into view from the other side like a prop on a stage, his body populating for her piece by piece as the metal curtain lifts. His gentle chestnut eyes grow brighter as he notices Zoe waiting patiently on the dock and smiling back at him.

"Hello again!"

Zoe nods in acknowledgment and continues.

"So, how is the crew at Metropolitano treating you?"

He beams.

"Oh, quite well, everybody is great. Thank you for your referral."

Zoe smiles.

"I knew you'd fit right in. So, what do you have for us today?"

He answers just as Amber comes up behind her.

"A couple cold packages. They're pretty big. I can give you a hand if you need."

Amber interrupts the warm exchange, reaching down from the platform's edge to hand the tablet with the inventory and release forms back to him.

"Here you go. All set."

Zoe dismisses herself with a squeeze at Amber's shoulder,

"I think I can manage; see you this weekend. Bye, Antonio!"

The cold room is Amber's favorite place and Zoe's least favorite. She doesn't know how Amber spends so much time in there without her fingers or her limbs or her brain freezing. She can only manage a couple of hours at a time in spite of all the weather gear she piles on. She preps Amber's workstation, rolling her case cart between two parallel surgical tables and placing two kick buckets underneath each one, as well. Amber strolls in with a trolley cart of packages, stacked one on top of the other, and sets them by the table. She picks one up and beckons Zoe.

"Come, I want you to see these."

Amber grabs a pair of surgical scissors and gloves from the cart. She hastily slips on the gloves and carefully cuts open the package to reveal a pair of incredibly pristine human hands sawed off precisely two inches below the wrist. They are perfect, almost too perfect to be human. Amber looks over to Zoe, her face aglow with satisfaction.

"They're beautiful, aren't they?"

Zoe blushes and can't help but smile, noticing the passion in Amber's dark, wild eyes.

"They're absolutely perfect."

Each of them takes a hand, examining them in rapture, cataloging the details.

1 . the digits are solid, uniform, smooth, just the right size
2. the fingernails are cut short, square, bits of lunula visible at the cuticles
3. the veins seem strong, durable—they should manage the integration well

Amber runs her index finger down the middle of one, from the tip of the median digit to the base of the palm. She traces the flexion creases, the young calluses above them. She closes her eyes. Sighs. She can almost feel the life in it, taste it, a finger in her mouth, on her tongue.

They are beautiful.

They are perfect.

He is a fly on the fucking wall.

All he can do is watch her, follow her scent, from room to room, limb to limb. All he can do is let obsession consume him, stalk the impossible grace of her movements as she loses herself in the skill of it all — the art of the scalpel running across frigid skin, disrobing it. The peony flesh that lies beneath is putty in her hands, sculpting clay. She plays with strings, fusing dismembered things with sutures, silk at her fingertips. The careful rhythm of her needle's repair work is poison in his veins, metamorphosis.

she is a black widow, a mad butcheress

a weaver of nightmares, of transformation
he is her prey, her meal, a satisfaction
he dreamt he was a man
the dream is over now
the room is spinning, closing in around him, his mind
he is falling apart, missing limbs
he is a sum of broken parts
useless eyes, tunnel vision
thoughts, memories, mutilation
teeth, nails
appendages where they shouldn't be
all of a sudden
he can see
Is he dying?
Is this how it happens?

Creation is a right reserved for those desperate and desolate enough to seek it. She can't stop, can't sleep. She wouldn't be able to stop if her life depended on it.

Zoe is gone for now. Amber is electric.
He will live.
He is a fly on the fucking wall
but not for long
The dream has the lifespan of a fly.
What is the lifespan of a fly?

She builds him up strong, winding gauze tight around the neat patchwork limbs like skeins of spider silk.

He is an insect
tangled in her web, trapped in Amber again.
She is God.
She is everything.

Amber's aching hands hover gently over the tenderly encased parts of the makeshift corpse beneath her layers of gossamer. Her cool olive skin is nearly devoid of color now from the cold, a victim too of the warmth she continues denying it. Her fingers are barbed ghosts—sharp shells of what they once were—in need of blood, consciousness, desire, hope—same as her creation, same as the fly on the wall.

All he can do is watch her,
strain his useless gaze to capture her agony,
pay testimony to her torment, her tears.
They stream down the frozen hillside of her cold, calcified
features.
All he can do is see them trickle past her neck to her collarbone
and collect in the grooves,
form puddles, pools he wishes to dive into.
She is an angel in the marble of his universe, his point of view.

He is still just a fly on the fucking wall.

Scriptures of the dead men she grew up worshipping say even God rested on the seventh day when his creation was complete when he saw that it was good. But tonight is no seventh day in Eden for Amber. Her reproduction is not complete. Her creature is heartless, headless, hopeless.

She is out of time.

There is a storm brewing outside, the one Antonio warned her of. The skies growl in apocalyptic applause as the rain nears. First, one drop, then another, and another. They batter the roof of the facility, soak the soil beneath it, run down its walls, lulling her to sleep against her will, like a symphony, a song of bludgeoning—like the beating of a missing heart, like the blood pumping through its chambers —teeming with blood, so much blood.

It pools at her feet.

Amber collapses in a heap of depleted flesh over the operating table—over her headless, heartless, lifeless dream. Her frigid arms cling to him nonetheless, cuddle him to her breasts.

Instinct.
He is dying.
This is how it happens.
He watches it all in spite of his decomposition, fighting every step of the way, fighting for his life.
He is an insect.
A Fly.
What is the lifespan of a fly?

The doorbell rings and rings again. Amber doesn't hear it; she wouldn't hear it if she could…if she had a choice. Zoe's fist pounds the door as she chimes in,

"Amber! Open up!"

But there is no pounding in her skull today, no sense of urgency.

Only doubt. Only insecurity. Only defeat.

Only the weight of her sorrow.

The blood on her hands, at her feet.

Confession: The cold is a terrible thing to get accustomed to.

Antonio's voice blossoms from beyond the security gate, trickling down the hallway like morning dew, the only life in the graveyard silence of the concrete Eden. Zoe's voice trails behind.

Their voices are like memories.

The voice of the operating system follows.

Manual Override Successful.
Access Granted.

Antonio taps his foot anxiously in the wintry corridor as he waits for Zoe to return from the cold room. He brings his hands up to his lips, breathes into them, and rubs them together, forcing warmth from the friction. A faint buzzing alerts him to a fly on the wall. He stares at the creature who seems to stare back at him, wondering why he feels so strange all of a sudden, so out of place, so alien.

Coming here was a mistake.
The cold white walls in stark contrast with the darkness

He can't take his eyes off the insect that can't seem to take its eyes off of him—the fly on the wall. Its compound eyes bore into him, his mind, luring him, entrancing him, trapping him in its gaze. He fights it, forces himself to look away, mutters under his breath.

*"That's not a normal **fucking** fly."*

There's something different about it, something unnatural. He looks over to the open gate, the sunshine pouring through, the breeze, steeling his nerves, and calls out for her.

"Zoe! Is everything ok in there?"

A tickle at his earlobe answers him. His hand instinctively snaps at it. His eyes dart back to the wall where the fly is. It's gone. He scans the hallway frantically, his skin crawling with the unease of the alien moment. It seizes him. They're inside him, his flesh. He can feel them in there, squirming, teeming, growing, taking over. He panics. Screams.

"ZOE!"

Zoe finds Amber bent over her patchwork lover, cradled in his arms, warm as death. She swipes a strand of Amber's dark hair from her face and slips it behind her ear, cups her cool face with her free hand, then leans forward and whispers,

Wake up, Amber.
Open your eyes.
It's time.

Amber opens her eyes.
Rises.
As they exit the cold room, Amber turns toward the lab, her instincts on autopilot. Zoe turns to face the now fully immobilized Antonio. She smiles, runs her fingers from his temple down to his chin, and stares into his desperate eyes, the soft pools pleading for her mercy, nearly brimming now from their edge. She leans in, presses her cheek to his cheek, her lips to his catatonic ear, and whispers,

The rain is my favorite weather.

Did you know that about me?

Zoe cleans and preps the cold room, laying Antonio's body on the operating table immediately beside Amber's creation. She caresses the thrumming veins in both his arms before puncturing them to commence transfusion. She is enraptured by the life draining from him to his benefactor as the clear tubes connecting them turn scarlet. It pleases her, fills her, throbs in her skull. Her eyes roll back in response.

She cries out in ecstasy, and the weather mimics her, follows along.

Raindrops, first one, then another.

Streams, then rivers, then oceans.

They drip through a leak in the roof as night descends on Eden with the subtlety of thunder, lightning, a full moon, the perfect storm,

the perfect conditions.

Amber joins Zoe in the lab.

Ready when you are, my life.

Zoe embraces her.

Lighting strikes, and they are one again.

Amber's favorite Sinatra song rings alongside the now roaring thunder overhead.

"Fly me to the moon…"
Sinatra

She lives.

Lightning strikes again, the sky flooding the darkness with light.

Amber marches to a monitor at the entrance of the cold room and instructs the operating system in the formula's code—his heart, his mind, creation at her mercy.

The voice of the system responds.

"Running: Adam Sequence."

The roof breaks above her, parting like a mechanized red sea, powered by electricity instead of Moses's plea. The storm pours in, forming puddles at her feet as she walks toward the center of the room, toward her dream—creation. Thunder roars in her skull.

It will change the world as we know it.

Beneath the deluge, she is God again, a deity, omnipotence. Amber severs Antonio's head after admiring it one last time. She gazes into the soft, warm brown eyes. His irises always reminded her of dried tobacco leaves, the color of the scent on his lips, his breath. She closes her eyes and traces the protrusion in his neck with her fingernail, remembering the night they met and his ridiculous attempt to humor her as he handed her an apple martini.

"An apple a day keeps the doctor away," he'd remarked with a smile.

She shakes her head and washes the memory away with a click of her teeth.

Confession: Life is a terrible thing to get accustomed to.

Her weaving hands needle into his flesh, sculpting it to her creation, completing the ritual, the incarnation, thread by macabre thread, each stitch more effortless than the rest. They slice open his chest, slip through the bones imprisoning the life within, pull out the beating heart, bury it in the gaping wound at her creature's breast, as if it were easy, as if she had done it a thousand times, as if she had never failed—would never fail again.

The moon shines overhead, casting a blessing of light over their
unholy trinity.
An insect spins concentric circles beneath the night, invading
Eden
Not by nor against his will
He owns no will but hers, and it will be done regardless of
what it costs him, his mind, his body, his spirit
a centrifuge, a vortex, a black hole,
birthed of her sorrow, her need, her desire, her blasphemy,
limitless, voracious, inescapable.
He is hers, her willing slave, her dream, her sacrifice.
All else be damned.
Her will be done.

Lightning strikes the fly like a bullet to the head, obliterating what is left of the insect and carrying him directly into the heart of Amber's creation. He is nothing but a speck amidst the crimson—a dot, but not for long. His obsidian nature bleeds into the embroidered man-like ink onto a blank canvas. He is a drip of consciousness, a stream of thought, a storm of recollection, a flood. He turns scarlet blood to ebony in his veins, but not without a fight. Every step of the way, the cells scream torture in futile resistance to death, to life. He convulses with change, the blackened cruor seeping through his bandaged wounds in blotches. Amber's eyes glow beneath the moonlight with madness, with satisfaction, as she witnesses the gruesome transformation. She smiles, and her teeth glisten in the dark, waiting for him to open his eyes to see her.

He opens his eyes.
He rises.
He is alive.
She is God.
She is everything.

——————END

colorín colorado, este cuento se ha acabado

— OLD SPANISH SAYING

poetry

POESÍA

maríangula

(GIVE ME BACK MY TONGUE)

there's a shallow grave behind a cornfield,

just over yonder
yonder

a hole dug in the soil by nimble claws
ripe with wounds and hushed incantations

María Angula, María Angula

vowed at the tender age of twenty
there's a cadaver buried
under a tombstone of wildflowers with daisies in its eye
sockets
a dagger in its hollowed-out womb
and the nectar of peony buds where there used to be a
tongue

mi lengua

(my tongue)

just over yonder,
yonder

there's a paranormal force, a ghost resurrected by its dese-
cration

María Angula, María Angula

devuélveme mi lengua
(give me back my tongue)

Ni puta, Ni pura, Ni tuya
(not whore, nor pure, nor yours)

mía, mía, todavía
(mine, mine, still mine)

there's a cemetery in my backyard
beneath fruiting vines *and hierbabuena* (sweet mint)
a crucifix composting in the garden with memories of Eden,
of expulsion
carved into its pulpy, putrid, proud paper flesh
wood carcass of Pinocchian nature
"I want to be a real boy," it says

(weeds don't die, they seed
that's what my mother used to say to me———before dying)

there's a man inside a whale, a woman inside a clamshell

just over yonder,
yonder

devuélveme mi lengua
(give me back my tongue)

María Angula.

Ni puta, Ni pura. Ni tuya.
(not whore, nor pure, nor yours)

maríangula

(DEVUELVEME MI LENGUA)

Hay una tumba, poco profunda detrás de un campo de maíz,

un poco más allá de aquí
más allá de aquí

un agujero excavado en el suelo por ágiles garras
repleto de heridas y hechizos susurrados

María Angula, María Angula

prometida, a la tierna edad de veinte años
hay un cadáver enterrado bajo una lápida de flores silvestres,
con margaritas en las cuencas de sus ojos
una daga en el lo hueco de su vientre
y el néctar de capullitos de peonía donde solía estar la lengua

mi lengua
(my tongue)

                              un poco más allá de aquí
                                    un poco más allá

existe una fuerza sobrenatural, un fantasma resucitado por
su profanación

            María Angula, María Angula

                              devuélveme mi lengua
                              (give me back my tongue)

                              Ni puta, Ni pura, Ni tuya
                              (not whore, nor pure, nor yours)

                              mía, mía, todavía
                              (mine, mine, still mine)

hay un camposanto en mi patio
bajo enredaderas fructíferas y hierbabuena
un crucifijo haciéndose abono en el jardín con recuerdos del
Edén, de la expulsión
tallado en su carne de papel, pulposa, podrida y orgullosa
cadáver de madera, y alma de Pinocho
"quiero ser un niño de verdad, dice"

                      (la mala hierba no muere, se crece
                  eso decía mi madre——antes de morir)

hay un hombre dentro de una ballena, una mujer dentro de
una concha

un poco más allá de aquí
un poco más allá

devuélveme mi lengua
(give me back my tongue)

María Angula.

Ni puta, Ni pura. Ni tuya.
(not whore, nor pure, nor yours)

libre

(YO SOY, I BE)

Yo Soy.

I am. I am

del sol, la luna, del mar.
(of the sun, the moon, the sea)

I be.

Libre

(free)

stride by stride
The morning star tans my hide
neptune whips my thighs
with freedom.

Libre

Soy Yo. Yo Soy.

                                                    I am. I be.

                        Ni Puta, Ni Pura.
                        Ni Puta, Ni Pura.
                        Ni Puta, Ni Pura.

                                                    Not half.
                                                    Nor whole.
                                                    Nor whore.
                                                    Nor pure.

Suya, Suya, Tuya.

                                    Yo soy.
                                    I am.
                                    I be.

pétalo de rosa
rose petals in his hand
bloomed of his rays
of the sun
his flame
his reign

                                                    lluvia en sus manos
                                                    rain in her arms
                                                    wild bent to her will

of the moon

depth sanctified in she, in sea.

Soy

I be

Libre

(free)

Soy yo. Yo soy.

I am. I be.

caballera, jinete, alma, maldita, bendita, soy

you knight-mare, horse rider, unholy, holy ghost
a little heaven, a little hell, a lot of heathen

Eden
Godiva
lightning-veined, moon child
Hija de la Luna.

Del Sol.
(Of Sun)
Del Mar.

(Of Sea)

Soy yo. Yo soy.

I am.

I be

Ni Puta. Ni Pura.
Ni Puta. Ni Pura.
Ni Puta. Ni Pura.
Poeta.
Poetisa.
Poesia.

suya, suya, tuya

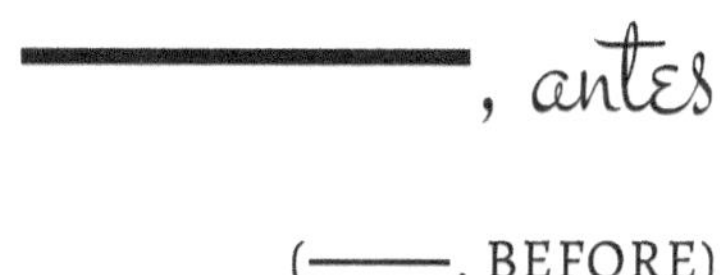

(——, BEFORE)

before the boot, there was the sole

antes de la bota———la planta de los pies

before the light, the endless dark

antes de la luz———la eterna oscuridad

before the saints, the stars

antes de los santos, las estrellas

ch'askakuna ñawikuna
(the stars, the heavens in our eyes)

there was the soil, with her infernal core

la tierra libre antes del eden

the soul, her whisper in the shadow of the morn

el alma, su susurreo en la sombra del amanecer

kay pacha Inti (the sun of the world)
kay pacha Quilla (the moon)
kay pacha alman (the soul)
qispisqa kay (the free———dom)

before the ark, the ship, the wild sea

antes de la arca, el barco, el mar

before the home, the dream, the shore

antes de la casa, el sueño, la costa

Madre Mar
Yemaya, Atabey, Mama Qucha

before Babylon's towers, there was the seed

antes de la torre de Babel, la semilla

the forest, the giant tree

el bosque, el árbol gigantesco

there was the peak, the summit

la cumbre

the sleeping titans in the green

    los titanes dormidos dentro de lo verde bajo el sol

        anti suyu urqukuna
        (The Andes)

before the plane, the bird, the vulture

    antes de avion, las aves, el buitre, el guaraguao

        el Huracán
        (the hurricane)
        las nubes en blanco y negro y gris
        (the clouds, all light and dark and in-between)
        y el cielo azul azul
        (the sky so blue, so true)

before the lie, there was a truth, a sight

    antes de la falsedad, la verdad, la perspectiva

the earth, the sky

    la tierra, el cielo

in you, your eyes

    en ti, en tus ojos

Ch'askakunamanta Awkikuna
(ancestors of the stars)

how I have searched for you.

trenza

(TRENZANDO LA NOCHE)

De mi trenza brotó una canción, un himno, y decia asi
la selva vive en ti
de ti, por ti

hay un lugar que conozco, donde voy
donde cantamos himnos al son del río Chone
y los enviamos por los arroyos desde las montañas hasta el mar
(a Bahia)

donde enterramos nuestros dedos en la arena
y hacemos un aro del tiempo, de nuestro tiempo

Trenza
(trenzando la noche)

y mientras la luna hace plata de tu piel
cobre de la mía

Tu eres mia
Yo soy tuya
El mundo es de nosotras

Trenzo la noche a tu cabello
como solías hacer con el mio
y nada se queda sin decir
no hay nada de qué arrepentirse

la sombra no le pertenece a la muerte
la luz nunca ha sido su ausencia

Trenza
(trenzando)

sigues ahi
todos siguen aquí

todos tan mios
todos tan libres

el viento sobre mi trenza

la luna

la cordillera

la marea

la tormenta

el dorado **choclo** *del amanecer*

y se
cuando abra los ojos
la huilota volverá a cantar

cucurrucucu, paloma

(regresare a ti)
la selva vive en ti
de ti, por ti

Trenza

trenza

(BRAIDING THE NIGHT)

Of my braid, there spilled a song, a hymn, and it went
like this
the wild lives in you
of you, for you

                                        there's this place I go, I know
                        where we sing hymns to the tune of the river *Chone*
                send them down streams that run from the mountains to
                                                                the sea
                                                              (a Bahía)

where our naked toes are buried in the sand
in a loop of time, our time

                            Trenza
                        (braiding the night)

. . .

and as the moon lights up your pale skin to silver
my olive to a shade of ore

You are mine
I am yours
The world is ours

I braid the night into your hair
the way you did with mine
and nothing is ever left unsaid
there's nothing left to regret

the shadow does not belong to death
the light has never been an absence of it

Trenza
(braiding the night)

you are there
you are all there, with me

all so mine
all so free
the wind over my braid
moon
mountain
sea
and roaring storm

the golden ***choclo*** of the dawn

and I know
when I open my eyes
the mourning dove will be cooing again

cucurrucucu, paloma

I will return to you

Trenza

pandora

(DESDE ANTES QUE NACÍ)

yo pienso que te he extrañado desde antes que nací
que los poetas no envejecen con el tiempo
que se hacen niños otra vez
y pienso
que he sido vieja desde antes que nací
desde antes que los dioses que maldijeron a Pandora tuvieran
la oportunidad de alcanzarnos,
de darnos la maldición
y que pelar yuca a los seis años me hizo anciana
porque en días como este, yo me acuerdo de tu sonrisa, de tu
risa a carcajadas,
de pecadora, de inocente
y tu recuerdo parece ser más niña de lo que yo fui
y hago todo color de rosa a pesar de la verdad
con la sangre de tu matriz, tus entrañas, sal de tus ojeras, mar
que vive en mi
todas mis recetas son tuyas, paloma, poeta, poetisa
y todas aún me recuerdan a ti

yo pienso
que te he extrañado

desde antes que nací

pandora

(SINCE BEFORE I WAS BORN)

I think I've missed you since before I was born,
that poets do not get older with time
that they become children again
and I think
I've been old since before I was born,
since before the gods that cursed Pandora had the chance to
touch us,
to bless us with their curses.
I think
peeling cassava root at six years old made me ancient because
on days like these, I remember your smile, your raucous
laughter,
it's sinfulness, it's innocence
and your memory feels more girl than mine was
and I tinge everything rose despite the truth
with the blood of your womb, your gut, the salt of your dark
circles, sea that lives in me.
All of my recipes are yours, dove, poet, poetess

and all still remind of you
I think
I've missed you

since before I was born

el cuento del sol, la luna, y el arcoiris

Erase una vez
el sol, con su fulgor en plena soledad
le pregunto a la luna negra de la oscuridad
por su bondad
si quería ser amiga suya y ella respondió
claro, como no?
y gracias por preguntar
y si me obsequias unos rayos tuyos, veras
cómo los reflejaré sobre la tierra, sobre el mar
y brillaré tu luz por ti
sobre toda criatura que la desconoce
y el sol al escuchar, como se puso a llorar
lloro tanto, en realidad
que las nubes parieron el arcoiris
para obsequiarselo
y desde ese entonces
el sol persiguió a la luna con su bondad
tras el cielo azul

tras las montañas, tras los valles, tras los rios
sin descansar
y así llenaron la tierra de los arcoiris

de amor

the story of the sun, the moon, and the rainbow

once upon a time
the sun, in all his brilliant solitude
asked the night's black moon
for her benevolence
if she would be his friend, and she replied
sure, why not?
and thank you for asking
and if you bestow on me some of your rays, you'll see
how I will reflect them over the earth, the sea
and shine your light for you
over every creature it does not see
and the sun, how he cried so
he cried so much, in fact
that the clouds birthed the rainbow
as a gift
and from that moment on
the sun chased the benevolent moon
across the brilliant blue

across the mountains, the valleys, the rivers
without repose
and thus, they flooded the earth with rainbows

with love.

cosecha

(A REAPING)

I reap what I *sow.*

I come bearing

Life.
Death.
Garden.
Fruit.

Yo cosecho lo que siembro.
Amor.
Muerte.
Vida.
Sabor.

I reap what I *sow.*

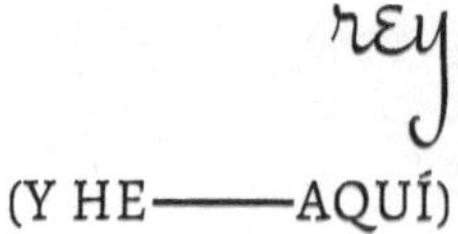

(Y HE——AQUÍ)

y he——aquí

allí, en tierra fértil y santo pastar
cómo crece la selva, aún
el verde largo del diente de león, la rosa, la zorra
la serpiente, barrigona, y valiente
y digiriendo aún el ámbar de nuestros ojos
vista, semilla, tendón

...y asi ha de ir

y he——aquí

allí, si estiras la nuca hacia el sol

Principito, Rey

cómo gruñe aún el cielo bajo el rubio del sol
en desfile de trueno, relampago

todo lleno de sal, de mar
y el peso de todo lo conocido
todo aún por conocer
cuán lejos hemos llegado del ayer
y cuánto nos queda por correr

...y asi ha de ir

y he———aquí

allí, en mar áspero, espumoso
como en pie de lucha sigue la vela, aún
torre distante en el azul, acarreando aguja, aún

remando, remando, aún
cuán lejos hemos llegado del ayer

y he———aquí

cómo cantan los grillos, aún
hierve en la olla, la hierba———buena, aún
sobre las llamas, aún
y un mensaje suena
sobre el tendido del teléfono

...y asi ha de ir

y he———aquí

rey

(AND LO——————BEHOLD)

and lo————behold

there in verdant pasture and shaded loam
how yet the wild grows
the long green legs of dandelions, the fox, the rose
the snake, all full bellied and brave
and yet digesting the amber of our eyes
sight, seed, and sinew

...so it goes

and lo————behold

there, if you crane your neck up toward the sun

Principito, Rey
(little prince, king)

how yet the sky growls 'neath the gilded star

in thunderous rows
all full of salt and tide
and the weight of everything known
yet to be known
how far we've come from home
how far we've yet to go

...so it goes

and lo———behold

there in the broken sea, the foam
how yet the sail stands tall
lone tower in the distant blue yet hauling marlin

row, row, rowing boat
how far we've come from home

and lo———behold

how yet the crickets chirp
the sweet grass rolls to a boil in the pot
over the fire
and a message rings
on a telephone wire

...so it goes

and lo———behold

la amistad

(FRIEND——SHIP)

en la lengua de mi madre
(in my mother tongue)
(my mother's tongue)

Saint Valentine's day is a day of
(el dia de San Valentín es)

love **and** friendship
del amor **y** la amistad

I always get hung up on that last word

Friendship
Friend——ship

La Amistad

: a 19th century two-masted schooner owned by a Spaniard
(un español, joder)
living in Cuba

mutiny

at open sea

rebellion
justicia
lealtad

rebellion
justice
loyalty

esas cosas me importan a mi
those things matter to me
to me, to me, to me

a mi

a-la-ru-ru-gata
(CANCIÓN DE CUNA)

me sigo quedando dormida——levantándome
despertando
a una canción de cuna

> *"a-la-ru-ru-gata"*
> *hush*
> *muñequita*
> *(little baby doll)*
> *el tiempo es tuyo, todo el tiempo del mundo*

Y al sonido de la pantalla del televisor tocando animados de
los noventas.
¿En qué parte de la tierra se encuentra Carmen San Diego?

> *Mommy?*
> *Mami?*

tuve una pesadilla
me desperte llorando y tu no estabas

yo era una niña sin cara
hecha de cráneo, de cabello
la televisión
tocaba animados de los noventas

a repetición.

En algún lugar...

...en la distancia
escuchaba sonar canciones de amor, españolas

carreteras

——a ningun lugar.

tenía miedo de nunca volverte a ver
se me acababa el tiempo

la carretera

el roble
la tierra.

el mundo se volvió plano como una pantalla.
y yo corría hacia el borde de ella
no pude evitar el subir y bajar de mis piernas,
los ángulos de 90 grados de su voluntad
mis pies, de dar contra el suelo

y tu no estabas.

me sigo quedando dormida
despertando
a una canción de cuna

carreteras

——a ningun lugar.

"a-la-ru-ru-gata, que parió una gata,
doce borriquitos, y una garrapata"

Sigues allí
aqui

"a-la-ru-ru-gata"
(hush)
muñequita
(little baby doll)
el tiempo es tuyo, todo el tiempo

...del mundo.

(you've got all the time...

...in the world).

a-la-ru-ru-gata

(A LULLABY)

I keep falling asleep——getting up
waking up
to a lullaby,

"a-la-ru-ru-gata"
hush
little baby doll
(muñequita)
you've got all the time in the world
(el tiempo es tuyo, todo el tiempo del mundo)

And the sound of a tv screen playing 90's cartoons.
Where on earth is Carmen San Diego?

Mommy?
Mami?

I had a nightmare.
I woke up crying and you weren't there.

                              I was just a girl without a face,
                           just the back of my head and hair
                                             the tv screen
                                         played 90s cartoons

on repeat.

Somewhere...

                                          ...in the distance
                             I could hear Spanish love songs

carreteras

                                           ——to nowhere.

                      I was scared I might never see you again.
                                   I was running out of time,
                                               of road,

de carretera

                                                  of oak,
                                                  of soil.

                      The earth became flat like a tv screen
                        and I was running to the edge of it.

I couldn't stop my legs from moving
in 90 degree angles bent to their will
my feet from battering the ground
and you weren't there.

I keep falling asleep,
waking up
to a lullaby

"a-la-ru-ru-gata"
hush
little baby doll
(muñequita)
you've got all the time in the world.

It wasn't fair.
None of it was ever fair
but I can still hear your laughter in the air,
your lullabies,

carreteras

——to nowhere.

"a-la-ru-ru-gata, que parió una gata,

doce borriquitos, y una garrapata"

You're still there,
here.

> *hush*
> *(a-la-ru-ru-gata)*
> *little baby doll*
> *(muñequita)*
> *you've got all the time...*

>> *...in the world.*

>> *(el tiempo es tuyo, todo el tiempo*

>> *...del mundo).*

diente de león

(¿SABIAS?)

¿SABIAS?

La raíz de cúrcuma produce hojas verdes, suaves que saben un poco como una mezcla entre el clavo de olor y el cebollín y también un poco a hierbabuena, la que crece junto al fregadero.

¿Y SABES?

Odio recordar lo triste que es olvidar el sonido de voces que ya no están y que la alegría es más fácil de recordar que el llanto, pero como sea, te hace llorar.

¿SABIAS?

El té de menta sabe aún mejor con miel, y también en los días fuera de la época de Navidad, y que me hace echar de menos a un momento perfecto que no fue perfecto para ti pero si lo fue para mí. Eso te lo agradezco.

¿Y SABES?

Una bellota es un amuleto cuando la regalas bajo una luna llena con toda la intención de tu corazón.

¿SABIAS?

Siempre pienso en ti, tu sonrisa, tu luna.

¿Y SABES?

Los volcanes se erosionan y hacen que las arenas a su alrededor se vuelvan negras como la noche—
Que esa arena brilla como el sol y arde igual de caliente y—
Que es la arena más bonita que he visto en mi vida.

¿Y SABIAS?

Que las abejas son tan gentiles como los lepidópteros a pesar de su picada—
Que se apoyen a lo largo de los manglares junto al mar y construyan imperios de sus árboles—
Que yo las amo por eso.

¿Y SABES?

Las conchas me hacen pensar en el luto de la mañana, de
ciertas mañanas, y del asesinato de Hipatia—
pero no simultáneamente, con la excepción de dias—
en los que me pongo a desempolvar y encuentro una concha
en donde mi madre escribió la palabra "sabiduría" con un
marcador plateado.

¿Y SABIAS?

Aun amo a las muñecas y siempre he odiado conducir, a
menos que el camino esté vacío, con rumbo a ningún lugar,
...o quizás
dirigido hacia un campo donde florece la selva en diente de
león, en soles que abrazan la tierra, un tanto antes de crecer
piernas
largas, verdes
y cabezas blancas, suaves...
...explosivas
...fragiles
...eternas

llenas de los deseos del amanecer

root

(DIENTE DE LEÓN)

DID YOU KNOW?

Turmeric root grows soft green leaves that taste a little like a
mix between cloves and scallions
and also a bit like the hierba buena growing by the sink.

AND DO YOU KNOW?

I hate remembering how sad it is to forget the sound of
someone's voice, and how joy is easier to recall than tears but
it also makes you cry.

DID YOU KNOW?

Peppermint tea tastes even better with honey, and when it's
not Christmas, it reminds me of a perfect moment that was
not perfect for you but was for me. Thank you for that.

DID YOU KNOW?

An acorn is an amulet when you gift it beneath a full moon
with a full intention in your heart.

DID YOU KNOW?

I always think about you, your smile, your moon.

DID YOU KNOW?

Volcanoes erode and make the sands around them black as
night—
That it shimmers in the sun and burns just as hot—
That it's prettier than any other sand I've ever seen in my life.

AND DID YOU KNOW?

Bees are as gentle as lepidopterans in spite of their sting—
That they brace themselves along the mangroves by the sea
and build empires of trees—
That I love them for it.

DID YOU KNOW?

Shells make me think of mourning, of particular mornings
and of the murder of Hypatia—
but not simultaneously, except when I'm dusting—

and find one my mother wrote the word "wisdom" on with
a silver sharpie.

AND DID YOU KNOW?

I still love dolls
and I've always hated driving
unless the road is empty, going nowhere
...or maybe
only headed to fields where dandelion roots bloom suns to
embrace the earth
before growing long green legs
and soft, white heads...
...explosive
...fragile
...eternal

full of wishes for tomorrow

puntería

(POETA)

El poeta solo busca apuntar fijo, verdadero
disparar

Flecha a la cabeza------------------------> la semilla
directo, al seno del ave
de la bestia
cucurrucucu

La flecha busca renacer, morir...

—-aprender a vivir
—-vivir

Yo creo que el poeta reencarna en la puesta del sol, el
amanecer, las olas del mar, pétalo de flor, y tal vez en la voz
del viento, pero jamás más en cuerpo y piel.

y creo que soy poeta
y que esta sera la ultima version de mi piel

(y tambien se)

El poeta no es poeta sin su puntería, sin su precisión.

(see——ves)

La Poesía también es Puntería.
Poetry is also archery.

Flecha al corazón------------------------> al desangre.
    la herida busca libertad, sanidad

El poeta solo busca apuntar fijo, verdadero.
El poeta es la lengua de la herida.
Es la poesia.

Creo que la poesía hace que te broten ojos de los poros de tu piel y oídos de cada órgano por dentro de, con la excepción de la lengua y de los pulmones.

——porque de ahí proviene tu voz. Y tu voz es **TUYA**, más que cualquier otra cosa lo es.

(Y creo...)

(que yo también le pertenezco)

Yo creo que el poeta solo busca apuntar fijo, verdadero.

(——ser)

(——respirar)
(——apuntar)

------------------------->

☙ 105 ☙

(punteria)
(disparad)

shoot

(PUNTERIA)

The poet only aims to aim true
to shoot
disparar

    Arrow through the skull ------------------------> the seed
                Breast of the bird, the beast
                    cucurrucucu

                       The arrow aims to die, to be reborn

—-vivir
—-to live

*I think poets reincarnate in sunsets, the dawn, the tide, in
flower petals, and possibly, in the voice of the wind, but never
again in flesh and skin.*

*I think I am a poet
and that this will be the last version of my skin*

(and also, I know)

The poet is no poet without aim.

(see——ves)

Poetry is also archery.
La Poesía también es Puntería.

Arrow through the stone ----------------------> bleed.
the wound aims to be free, clean

The poet only aims to aim true.
*The poet **is** the tongue of the wound.*
***Is** poetry.*

I think poetry makes eyes pour out of every pore in your skin
and makes ears of every other organ within, with the excep-
tion of the tongue and of the lungs

——because that's where your voice lives. And your voice is
YOURS,
more than anything else ever is.

(and I think)

(that I belong to her too)

I think the poet only aims to aim true.

(to be——ser)

(to breathe——respirar)
(to aim——apuntar)

-------------------------->

(shoot)
(punteria)

llanto de llorona

(CANTO)

hundo mis dedos sedientos en la tela del espacio, el tiempo,
brecho mi universo
hago agujero en el ozono
un camino abandonado, avaro, sediento
rezo la paz que descansa en paz
la entierro en el oro arponeado de mi seno, mi verbo

mi canción

Llanto de Llorona
Canto

¿Qué más éxtasis que morir ahogado, amado?
¿Qué más tragedia que la profundidad sin explorar?

mi canción

Llanto de Llorona

anclada a tu cráneo, tu corazón
excava tu tesoro entre los escombros
encuentra el azul acero de un diamante perdido

la esperanza

Llanto de Llorona
Canto

hunde tus dedos sedientos en el tejido de mi universo, en mi
carne
haz de la muerte, de los torbellinos———una paradoja
traza el Triángulo del Diablo con tu lengua, descubre la
Atlántida

la perdición

y apaga tu sed en sal de mar

en Llanto de Llorona
Canto

has agujero en el ozono, crea camino
al purgatorio, al paraíso
¿Qué más éxtasis que morir ahogado, amado?

ven, ven
ven a mi

canto de llorona

(A WEEPING WOMAN'S SONG)

I dip my willing fingers in the fabric of space-time, breach
my universe
make a hole in ozone,
a forsaken path, full of greed, of thirst
pray peace may rest in peace
I bury her in my gold-harpooned breast, my word

mi canción,
(my song)

Llanto de Llorona
Canto

what greater ecstasy than death by drowning, dear?
what greater tragedy than depths left unexplored

mi canción,
(my song)

Llanto de Llorona

anchored in your skull, your heart,
dig for treasure among the wreckage, love
for the steel blue of a diamond lost at sea

la esperanza
hope

Llanto de Llorona
Canto

dip your willing fingers in the fabric of the universe, my flesh
make of all this dying, these maelstroms————a paradox
trace the Devil's Triangle with your tongue, discover
Atlantis,

perdition

and quench your thirst in saltwater, sea

en Llanto de Llorona
Canto

make a hole in ozone, a path
to purgatory, to paradise
what greater ecstasy than death by drowning, dear

ven, ven
won't you come here

rosa ametralladora

(DESPERADO)

Hay un sentimiento que ya casi no soporto en estos tiempos
(de necesidad, de avaricia, de hambre), que me hace pedazos
la piel, que se alimenta de la médula de mis huesos, y crea
agujeros en ellos, balaceras.

Antonio Banderas, el mariachi, en *Desperado, 1995*

y Salma Hayek en una librería, dueña, *rey.*

hay una canción dándome vueltas en la cabeza

rueda, rueda, rosas
un aroma

No soporto las palabras sencillas, ni las frases comunes, ni la
letra pequeña de los contratos
ni el menudo, ni el mondongo, ni la guatita.

No creo que lograré sacar el olor de hervir tantas vísceras de
mi nariz, jamás.

Ves
Yo provengo del mar (del caldo) que parió la poesía.

Y aun no soporto la manera que preparamos nuestras
propias vísceras para alimento
una piedra para tu olla, un tumba para tu ser, dos monedas
para el barquero, o tus ojos
receta de necesidad absoluta.
No soporto las necesidades.

No soporto cuanto necesito el mar.

(su aroma)

No soporto cuanto adoro las rosas.

(su aroma)

Ni mi adoración por una pueblo Mexicano, fronterizo,
donde conocí una carretera enorme, vacía...

Desperado

bailando

lambada, ae,

chingando

muriendo dignamente

Ametralladora
por pelotón de fusilamiento

                    punta- talon, pistola,

sangre de dios

toda roja, roja, llena de rosas,

hay una balacera en la médula de mis huesos aun

*muerte
deseo
pistola
sangre
roja*

Desperado

**Rosa
Ametralladora**

machine gun rose

(ROSA AMETRALLADORA)

There's a feeling I can't stand, can't seem to bear too long
these days (of need, of greed, of hunger), makes my skin
threadbare, feeds on the marrow of my bones, leaves bullet
holes.

Antonio Banderas, de mariachi, in *Desperado, 1995*

      and Salma Hayek in a bookstore, dueña, *rey.*

there's a song playing in my skull

> *ring around the roses*
> *a scent*

I can't stand...

    ...simple words, nor simple phrases, nor the fine print of
contracts anymore, nor the stewed intestines of the many
names I know *(mondongo, menudo, guatita).*

I don't think I'll ever get the scent of boiling guts clean out
of my nostrils.

See
I come from the sea (the soup) that birthed poetry.

and I still can't stand the way we prepare our entrails for
consumption,
a stone for your cauldron, a tomb for your soul, a coin for
the ferryman, or your eyes,
a recipe of absolute necessity.
I almost can't stand necessities.

I can't stand how much I need the sea.

(her scent)

I can't stand how much I adore roses.

(their scent)

Nor my adoration of a Mexican border town where I met
a big, empty, open road...

Desperado

dancing

lambada, ae,

fucking

dying an honorable death

Ametralladora
by firing squad

punta- talon, pistola,

sangre de dios

red, so red, replete of roses
toda roja, roja, llena de rosas,

there are bullet holes in the marrow of my bones,

muerte
(death)
deseo
(desire)
pistola
(pistol)
sangre
(blood)
roja
(red)

Desperado

Machine Gun
Rose

matador

(TE VOY A HECHIZAR)

Te voy a hechizar,
————————————> *matador*

a
elaborar
un vino tinto de mi piel
un sorbo carmesí
madurado en mi boticario
en salmuera de *amontillado* floreciendo rosa
dulce como la miel del   capullo de amapola
un ritual   en escarlata
como la *sangre*   que florece
del rubí de tu espada

Te voy a conjurar,
————————————> *matador*

empalar tu seno

tan pronto como el látigo de tu *muleta* me inspire hacerlo

atravesarte, tu pecho
y dejar un agujero enorme, *puto*
—————————————————> *matador*

sangrarte
de
t
o
d
a
t
u

sangre, degollado

que andes
sin corazon, por mi
que me importa a mi

Te voy a conjurar ——————————————> *matador*

de la nada, del aire libre
del fuego en las nubes
del viento sobre mi trenza.

—————————————> *matador*

matador

(I'M GOING TO CONJURE YOU)

I'm going to conjure you,
——————————————————> *matador*

by
brewing
a red drink of my flesh
a crimson sip of my skin
ripened in apothecary fashion
brined in *amontillado* till it's blooming roses
sweet as the milk of poppy buds
scarlet   rituals
like the *blood*   you brandish
ruby as your sword

I'm going to conjure you,
——————————————————> *matador*

charge at your breast

soon as the whip of your *muleta* inspires me to do so
impale you, your chest

and leave a gaping *fucking* hole where your soul used to be
——————————————> *matador*

bleed
y
o
u

sangrarte, degollado

you can walk around
without a heart for all I care,
for all I care

I'm going to conjure you ————————————> *matador*

of thin air
the fire in the clouds
the wind in my hair.

——————————————> *matador*

hazme poesia
(MAKE POETRY OF ME)

Hazme
Poesia
(make
poetry of me)
ven, vem,
come
malvado
(sinner)
pecador
ven

hazme poesia, en tus manos

(make poetry of me, in your grip)

from the tip of your fingers

(desde las puntas de tus dedos)

ink of your sword, blade, blooming, red

(la tinta de tu espada, afilada, floreciente, roja)

splinter the breast, fracture the stone

(astilla seno, quebranta piedra)

the soul

(alma)

again, again
(una y otra vez)
ven, vem
(come)
faça-me poesia
(make poetry of me)
llévame,
a tus brazos,
a tus fauces
(take me,
in your arms,
in your jaws)

wave willed of moon

(marejada de luna)

the gravitational pull that forms ——the tide

(la gravedad que crea ———la marea)

poetry

(poesia)

llámame, desármame

(beckon me, disarm me)

doblame a tu voluntad

(bend me to your will)

easy, so easy, good, so good,
(fácil, tão fácil, bom, tão bom)

easy as apple pie
tarta de manzana

atragántate de mi

(choke on me)

haz poesia

(make poetry)

drowned in me,

(ahogado en mi)

                                          die

(muere)

en llanto de llorona,

                                    in caustic rain

en lluvia, en melancolía

                              (in rain, in melancholy)

                              in milk of manzanillo

(leche de manzanillo)

                              come and come for me

(ven y ven por mi)

                              for murderous fruit

(por fruta asesina)

prohibida

                                          (forbidden)

                  lightning in the cotton of your mouth

(relámpago en el algodón de tu boca)

thunder in your fang

(trueno en tu colmillo)

nothing lost in translation

(nada perdido en la lengua)

vem,
vem,
malvado
vem
faça-me poesia
hazme poesia
come
make poetry of me
ven

merced

(BEG)

Merced, Merced, Misericordia.

beg
mercy
beg
pardon

of me, my heart, mother of woe, nail me to the cross

(de mi, mi corazón, madre de los dolores, crucifícame)

again
una y
otra vez
place
a crown
of thorns
upon my
head

lace it\
with roses\
rosas

so I\
may\
bleed\
for you\
again\
again\
meus deus\
deus meu\
my god\
beg

Merced, Merced, Misericordia.

Mercy, Mercy, Mercy.

beg\
beg\
beg\
beg\
beg

dancando lambada ae

(ROJA)

si fuese espada, aún sería pluma
y si fuese pluma, aun seria poeta
llena de muerte
——violenta, tierna, roja
tan roja, tan roja, tan roja

escribiría otro cuento trágico, mágico
de amantes centenarios
llegando a los cien
bailando
cogiendo

dancando lambada, ae

en medio de una carretera enorme, vacía
en el medio de la nada
con los buitres dando vuelta
sobre sus cabezas

son la noche eterna, esperando su turno a devorar

nuestros corazones latientes, nuestros ojos en blanco, y otras
partes

si fuese espada, aun seria pluma

————indomable

*esclava
de sus ordenes
de su muerte
de su nacimiento
del horizonte
carroña
fuego
humo
amanecer
amarilla
naranja
roja*

*tan roja
tan roja
tan roja*

dancando lambada ae

(RED)

if I were a sword, I'd be a pen
and if I were a pen, I'd be a poet
ripe with death
————violent, tender, red
so red, so red, so red

I'd scribble another tale of ruin, of loss
of nonagenarian lovers
nearing 100
dancing
fucking

dancando lambada, ae

in the middle of an open road
in the middle of nowhere
vultures circling
overhead

they are the night, waiting turn to devour

       beating hearts, rolling eyes, other parts

    if I were a sword, I'd be a pen

indomitable———indomable

in thrall
in service of
their death
the birth
of the horizon
carrion
made fire
smoke
sunrise
yellow
orange
red

so red,
so red,
so red

déshabillée

(DISCOVER ME)

discover me

(trouve-moi)

untamed, unashamed

(indompté, sans honte)

in the stalwart arms of willful willows

(dans les bras vaillants des saules délibérés)

discover me

(trouve-moi)

in full disregard of decorum

(dans un mépris total du decorum)

                    déshabillée
                    (disrobed)

leaves licking lust from between my thighs

                    (feuilles léchant le désir d'entre mes cuisses)

weeping

                                        (en larmes)

carry me away with the tide

                                (emporte-moi à la marée)

the flood

                                    (le déluge)

carry me astride

                            (prends-moi à califourchon)

into sin

                                    (dans le péché)

oh most impure

                                    (le plus impur)

there, you are mine

(là, tu es à moi)

there, I am yours

(là, je suis à toi)

α

(TATTOO)

I missed you once,
went to the ocean
felt you, your embrace
in the water, the wind
tasted you, your skin

piel de mi piel
(flesh of my flesh)
(skin of my skin)

licked my lips
salt, sea, and foam
shut my eyes
(cerré los ojos)
y todo se hizo espuma

aphros
(ἀφρός)
(foam)

(espuma)

product of the severed genitals of Uranus
birth of Aphrodite
sunlight
moonrise
tide

I rode
the space between your hips

**the fall of
Eden**

reverse cowgirl style
leaned over farther
your creation at my mercy

Cronus

tattooed a letter A onto your balls

*all scarlet sacrilege
Rose
all penance for your sins
Crimson
all absolute and everything
Encarnación*

diosa

(DE MARMOL)

quisiera ser
ningun heroe, ninguna bestia obediente
ninguna espada, ni caballeria prometida
quisiera dar
mi vida
por la mera oportunidad de tallarte del mármol
de dibujar
los valles de tus muslos de la piedra
partirlas
con las puntas de mis dedos, y llenar tu corazón sediento, de
mí, mi sangre
me gustaría
dejar atrás, más nada que el petricor de nuestras tormentas,
de nuestra lujuria
esparcido sobre las cenizas
de cualquier hombre
que se te oponga, diosa, ángel
para el gusto de los buitres, que prueben de tu fe
y despues

los mataría también
por sus pecados contra ti
si quisieras
y solamente, si
y únicamente, por ti

de marmol

(FOR THE ANGEL IN THE STONE)

I would like to be
no hero at your side, no noble beast
nor dutiful sword nor promised cavalry
I would like to give
my life
in exchange for the opportunity to carve you from marble
to draw
the valleys of your thighs from stone
part them
with my fingertips and pump your wanting heart full of me,
my blood
I would like to leave
behind nothing but the petrichor of our storms, our lust
strewn over the ashes, the dust
of any man
that dared oppose you, goddess, angel
for the vultures to enjoy, to taste your trust
and then,

I would slaughter them too
for their trespass against you
if you wanted me to
and only if
and only you

musa

(OF THE POET AND THE MUSE)

there is no freedom here
in this realm of skin and bone and order of the flesh,
carcasses

> *de carne, de muerte, de piel*
> *aquí no hay libertad, the poet says*

dream,

> *sueña*

do not speak to me of boundaries, of life

> *no me hables de la vida, de los límites*

things that can and cannot be done, be won
of rights, of wrongs

> *de aciertos, de errores, el bien, el mal*

floating salvation with wooden walls, of the buoyancy of her
cages
things of man, made of men

    de la salvación con paredes de madera, de la flotabilidad de
                                          sus jaulas
                   cosas del hombre, hechas por el hombre

          yo soy musa, diosa, tuya
          (I am muse, goddess, yours)

             yours

             I am
            tuya soy

I am a tattoo on your skin, your sex.

                    Soy tatuaje sobre tu piel, tu hombría

a pagan ritual ripped from your breast

                 un ritual pagano arrancado de tu seno

drown, choke on it, your blood

                    para ahogarte en ella, tu sangre

          Sangre de Dios

let me in, let me in

dejadme adorar
(let me adore)

let me win

I am a pillar of salt, the poem says

      Soy columna de sal, dice el poema

full of death,

        llena de muerte, de deseo

portraits, memories,

         retratos, recuerdos

warnings,

          consejos

war, will, fire, sea

       guerra, voluntad, fuego, mar

the sun, the moon, the fall

        el sol, la luna, la caída

the sacrifice

                                        el sacrificio

crucifixion of the light

                                        la crucifixión

the night

                                        la noche

flood,

                                        diluvio

                    destrucción,
                    (destruction)

                    renacimiento,
                    (rebirth)

if you are ocean, I am spume,

                              si tu eres mar, yo soy espuma

seafoam over blue

quicksand,

                              arena movediza

crucifixion of the light

sodium chloride in your wound

la sal de tus heridas

the crow, the olive branch, the sight, the seed

el cuervo, el ramo de olivo, la vista, la semilla

poesia
(poetry)

the poet seeks not the safety of the ark

el poeta no busca del arco, la salvación

earth, rock to land on,

to stand on

poets
swim
die
drown

el poeta nada,
se hunde en la profundidad
muere

bleed

sangra

salt

                                                            sal

   sea

                                                            mar

   red

                                                            rojo

musa
(muse)

como te deseo, cuanto te deseo
musa, libertad, amistad

do not speak to me of boundaries, of life

   no me hables de la vida, de los límites

of death, of fear

   de la muerte, del terror

things made of man, of men

   cosas del hombre, hechas por el hombre

Querida mia
(My dear)

they have yet no power here

aquí no tienen poder

come here, come here,
come here
ven, ven
c'mere, c'mere

everything will be alright

todo va estar bien

ven, ven
come here

lindor

(BON-BON DE FRESA)

the blood on your tongue
tastes of roses
insists some deaths are sweet, bon-bon de fresa

I sucked strawberry cream from a Lindor truffle while
watching a documentary on trees, how they speak, die, live,
breathe, bleed, are, be

> *magia, madera, roble, noble*
> *(magic, wood, oak, noble)*

I licked my chocolate-fresa lips, sunk my fingers in, closed my
eyes, dreamt of a world on fire with passion, the kind
heavy in the eyes of

> *la humanidad, humanos, robles, nobles*
> *(humanity, humans, oak, noble)*

who love trees instead of

war
anger
bloodshed

I tore the fabric of space-time
 again and again
defiant mortality
drip

chocolate-fresa

coursing through my veins

I sucked strawberry cream from a Lindor truffle, licked my
lips, closed my eyes, dreamt of

        roble (oak)

a world on fire with passion, the kind
heavy in the eyes of humans who love trees
instead of
war

       that is
       peace

       poetry

obrigada

eu quero

te obrigar
te obrigar, te obrigar

to compel you,
to face what you are
what you want

infernal, renascent angel
seething in your skin

o que calor
de luz, de sol, de pecador
obrigado a mim

to me, to me

for your transgressions, sinner

quero te obrigar
te obrigar
arrancar o seu coração

rip out your heart
drink up your vein

sangue de deus
meus deus
meus deus

oh
my god
my god

I'm going to drink up all your blood
drain you

drenar e drenar e drenar você

compel you
to face what you are
what you want

obrigado a mim
to me, to me
all thanks
to me

pandemonio
(PARA LA VAMPIRESA)

voy a hundir mis colmillos tan profundo en ti
las puntas perforarán el esófago, médula, toda vena, nervio,
tendón
responsables por tus pecados

pecador

voy hacerte beber tu propia sangre
ahogarte en ella
tu tentacion
tu sacrificio
voy a disfrutar cada minuto de tu lengua
torturada
rogando respirar
sangrarte

**Sangre de Dios
Blood of God**

rogando merced
mi placer

Tu Pandemonio

te voy arrancar los ojos
rodarlos en mi boca como chicles
partirte la cabeza por el medio
y desvestir lo de adentro

tus rosas,

y tomar lo que quiero

muerte y deseo

voy a desollarte
meterme en tu piel
ponermela de prenda sagrada

piel de mi piel

probarla
de vez en cuando

hierro y miel

voy a hundir mis colmillos tan profundo en ti

tentador

por tus pecados
hacerte
beber tu propia sangre
ahogarte
en ella

por tus pecados
hacerte
beber tu propia sangre
ahogarte
en ella

pandemonio

(FOR THE VAMPIRE QUEEN)

I'm going to sink my teeth so deep into your neck,
the tips will puncture esophagus, spinal cord, all veins,
tendons, nerves,
responsible for your transgressions,

sinner
(pecador)

I'm going to make you drink your own blood,
choke on it,

your temptation

(tu tentacion)

your sacrifice.

(tu sacrificio)

I'm going to enjoy every minute of your tortured tongue
gasping for breath,
blood.

Sangre de Dios
(Blood of God)

begging mercy of porcelain daggers,

(rogando merced)

my pleasure

(mi placer)

Tu Pandemonio
(Your Pandemonium)

I'm going to pop out your eyes,
roll them around in my mouth like gumballs,

crack open your skull,
disrobe proud peony flesh,

tus rosas,

(your roses)

and take what I want

⁞ 158

muerte y deseo
(death and desire)

I'm going to flay you
crawl into your skin,
wear it as holy garment

piel de mi piel
(skin of my skin)

taste it
every now and then,

hierro y miel
(iron, honey)

I'm going to sink my teeth in you

tempter
(tentador)

for your transgressions,
make you
drink your own blood
choke on it

Nos vemos, lengua
(See you around, tongue)

acknowledgments

I would like to thank, first and foremost, my publisher, Quill & Crow Publishing House, the whole team there, and Cassandra L. Thompson, my friend, my soul sis, my eternal inspiration for the opportunity and steadfast encouragement in setting so much of my voice free from its cage. Thank you for always believing in me.

I would also like to thank everyone in the community that has taken the time to read my work and reached out, commented on it, shared it, liked it, cheered me on, or encouraged me in any way. I am so grateful for all your support.

I share my work with the hope that it will grow in its reader the yearning for the many forms of liberation, of expression, of art, as poetry has always inspired in me. I would like to thank the poets, every poet, the art of poetry as a whole, because all of it has had a lasting impact on my spirit and I would not be who I am without it.

Thank you, all. I hope *My Split Tongue* serves you well and leaves you with nothing but a longing for more poetry.

A.L. Garcia is an Ecuadorian-American poet and writer currently based in Puerto Rico. She has contributed numerous stories to Quill & Crow anthologies over the years and has curated several of our Crow Calls poetry volumes. She belongs to the ocean, and her favorite flowers are dandelions.

thank you for reading

Thank you for reading *My Split Tongue // Mi Lengua Dividida*. We deeply appreciate our readers, and are grateful for everyone who takes the time to leave us a review. If you're interested, please visit our website to find review links. Your reviews help small presses and indie authors thrive, and we appreciate your support.

Other Poetry Titles by Quill & Crow

A Conjuring of Dandelions

Rise of the Dark Goddess

Crow Calls Volume VI